The Toad Men of the Caribbean

Justin Mitson

The Toad Men of the Caribbean

Contents

Dedication		**vi**
One	One	5
Two	Two	15
Three	Three	19
Four	Four	23
Five	Five	27
Six	Six	35
Seven	Seven	39
Eight	Eight	43
Nine	Nine	49
Ten	Ten	53
Eleven	Eleven	63
Twelve	Twelve	67
Thirteen	Thirteen	77
Fourteen	Fourteen	83
About the Author		**88**

To the amazing Zoe Wilson.

Minty, Snowy, and Goldie love you very much.
Thanks for being a Super-Fan.

May God richly bless you!

Red Team Ink
DBA of Zealot Solutions, Idaho LLC
9480 River Beach Lane
Garden City, ID 83714
Copyright © 2024 by Red Team Ink

This is a work of fiction. Names, characters, businesses, places, events, and incidents are either the products of the author's imagination or used in a fictitious manner. Any resemblance to actual persons, living or dead, or actual events is purely coincidental.

For permission requests or information about discounts for special bulk purchases please contact: redteamink@gmail.com. Substantial discounts on bulk orders are available to corporations, professional associations, and small businesses.

Printed in The United States of America
ISBN: 979-8-3304-3334-6
Title: The Toad Men of the Caribbean
Description: First Edition
Cover design by Donna Lane

{ one }

Snowy shivered as the *Gillfish 2* pulled away from the melting iceberg. She gazed at the crystal blue waters, smooth and fluid as they sailed toward England. Then she surveyed the deck. Captain Minty and First Mate Carter were engaged in conversation. Goldie giggled as she raced Claudette's daughters, Annelise and Camille. Claudette smiled warmly as she chatted with the other children. Clem, Rogers, and other members of the crew tended to their duties. Ivan and Evea, Carter's doves, were tucked into their cage near the ship's bow, their heads nestled into their feathers as they slept. Everything felt settled.

But Snowy was freezing as the sun sank on the horizon, so she went to the Duke of Somerset's trunk. Perhaps among the fancy dress-up clothes, jewelry, and wigs, she'd find something warmer. As she reached for the latch, a tiny blue spider crawled out.

"How odd," Snowy thought.

She watched it climb the trunk's lid. Its bright blue back glimmered in the last rays of sunshine reflecting off the water. Snowy leaned down for a closer look. Then she reached out, holding her chilly hand open.

"Come here, little one," she invited.

Shuffling its eight tiny legs, the blue spider crept toward Snowy's outstretched hand, then stopped.

"Aren't you so pretty?" she said, beckoning with her fingers.

The spider backed up but Snowy continued her coaxing.

"Don't worry," Snowy said. "I won't hurt you. I promise."

The spider slowly came forward, then climbed into Snowy's palm. When it did, Snowy's icy hand felt warm, even with the sea breeze beginning to pick up.

"Oh," she exclaimed. "You are the sweetest. Thank you for letting me hold you."

The spider tickled Snowy's palm, tucking its legs beneath it and settling down to sleep. Snowy gently folded her hand closed to keep the spider safe.

"What are you doing?"

Startled, Snowy looked up and saw Minty standing next to her.

"Oh," Snowy said, unfurling her hand. "Look at what I found."

Minty's eyes widened. "What is that and where did it come from?"

"A blue spider," Snowy declared. "It crawled out from under the lid of the duke's trunk."

Minty peered at the tiny arachnid. "I've never seen one like that. But speaking of the trunk," she said, jiggling the latch, "I hope there are some warmer things in here. I'm cold."

Snowy tried to help Minty lift the lid, but she struggled to keep her hand closed around the little spider.

"I've got it," Minty said, pushing the lid open. She combed through the items in the massive trunk, pulling out a few velvety capes lined with fur. She handed one to Snowy, who couldn't lift the heavy wrap with one hand. So, Minty draped it around her friend and fastened the shiny gold button through the loop at the neck.

"Thank you," Snowy said, instantly warmer and protected from increasing wind gusts.

"Now, let's see if we can find something …" Minty started as she rifled through the trunk again. "Ahh, this should work."

She produced a small match box and offered it to Snowy.

"What's this for?"

"Your spider's new home," Minty said, sliding the matchbox open. "Well, little one, what do you think of this?"

The spider remained still. Snowy worried that she might have harmed it, closing her hand around it too tightly.

"Oh no," she said. "Come on, spider."

Minty looked at Snowy, perplexed. With a slim finger, Minty stroked the spider's blue back. "Hey, little spider, wake up."

At her touch, the spider looked up and stretched out its legs.

"Oh!" Minty squealed. "It's so cute!"

Relieved, Snowy took the matchbox from Minty and placed it next to the spider. "Come on, spider."

Still, the spider stood remained motionless.

"Maybe it needs a name," Minty suggested.

Snowy looked at the spider. "Well, I get the sense it's a female. So, how about Ariadne?"

The spider wiggled in Snowy's hand.

"I'd say she likes that," Minty said. "Let's call her Ari for short. Ari, would you like to get out of the cold and into this nice warm box?"

The girls watched the tiny blue spider climb into the matchbox and settle back to sleep.

Snowy carefully closed the box and put it in her pocket. Then she yawned. "Sleep sounds like a good idea," she said.

"Go down and stretch out in one of the cabins," Minty said. "Carter and I know what to do."

"Are you sure? I should probably—"

"Go," Minty said, putting her hand on top of the velvet cape around Snowy's shoulders.

"I hope we go someplace warm after this," Snowy said, shivering again as she headed below deck.

***

After returning to England, the girls expected a visit from the Duke of Somerset. As Goldie, Annelise, and Camille played outside,

Claudette tidied up Snowy's cottage. Then she set about making a pot of chamomile tea.

When Snowy came down the stairs, she peeked through the tapestry drapes, just as the duke's carriage trundled up the path.

"He's here!" Snowy exclaimed, clapping her hands. "Oh, I hope Minty is on her way."

Claudette arranged the cups and saucers on a tray and Snowy threw open the door.

"Your grace," she said, "how nice to see you."

The duke dismounted from the carriage and greeted her with a handshake that turned into a hug. "Miss Snowy," he said, clasping his arm around her shoulders. "The pleasure is all mine."

Then he opened the carriage door to reveal Minty sitting inside.

"As you can see," he explained, "I swung by and collected Miss Minty since her cottage was on my way."

He offered Minty his hand as she stepped out. Then he reached back inside to retrieve a small package. Goldie and the other girls swarmed Minty, hugging her and giggling as they ran across the lawn.

"Well, that's a nice surprise," Snowy said. "And what's that?"

"You'll see," the duke said. "Shall we go inside?"

Claudette greeted them as they entered the cottage and motioned to the kitchen table, where she had set up the tea service. When the duke set the package on the table, it made a slight thud. Claudette served the tea, along with some of the madeleines from the recent trip. Then she excused herself to check on the girls playing outside.

"Well," the duke said, "you sent word of your grand adventure over the iceberg, traveling through several European countries at a time of war, and your subsequent defeat of Heinrich von Brock in order to rescue all these orphans, to Mr. Flamsteed, Sir Wren, and I at the Royal Observatory. It was then agreed that we should gift you a token of our appreciation. And, Miss Snowy, when you mentioned that you'd like to travel to someplace warmer, we thought this would make the perfect gift."

With that, he opened the package and pulled out a heavy, brass object. It had an odd shape, triangular with a curved bottom edge and what looked like a pair of small eyepieces attached.

"I've never seen anything like that," Snowy said, eyes enlarged. "What does it do?"

"Our friend and colleague, Isaac Newton—"

"SIR Isaac Newton?" Snowy blurted out.

"Yes," the duke said with a soft laugh, "he has earned the title. SIR Isaac Newton had been drawing this up. I believe he was inspired by the late Bartholomew Gosnold."

"A founder of Virginia Company," Snowy interjected. "He went to Jamestown, across the Atlantic, in the New World. He named a vineyard there after his late daughter, Martha. Gosnold died in 1607, the same year Johannes Kepler recorded the appearance and motion of a comet."

Minty nodded and sipped her tea.

"Correct," the duke continued, picking up the object and handing it to Snowy. "This little tool is handy for celestial navigation. Gosnold began developing it to measure the distance between an astronomical object and the horizon. Newton's been trying to perfect it. And this isn't completely accurate, but we think it will help you on your journey."

Snowy looked over the object, pushing her glasses up her nose. "Does it have a name?"

"We call it a sextant," Somerset replied, turning it over in Snowy's hand. "As you can see here, it also has a clock."

"Look at that," Snowy mused. "How fascinating."

The duke smiled. "We thought you'd like that. So, tell me, have you decided where you're going?"

Snowy handed the sextant to Minty, who began looking it over. "We thought the Caribbean might be a nice place to explore."

***

Minty stared at the gadget the duke had given them as the *G2* sailed toward the Caribbean. It was heavy and the brass glimmered in the midday sun. They'd left Claudette and the children, except Goldie, in Epping. Claudette had agreed to move into the unoccupied guest cottage on Snowy's property, in exchange for helping the girls. It was perfect for Annelise and Camille, and it was comforting to know someone would look after their cottages, and Galileo, while they were at sea.

They'd passed Ponta Delgada and the Azores, a Portuguese island chain in the North Atlantic, weeks ago and were now heading further southwest, past the New World, and beyond the Tropic of Cancer. Snowy had insisted on going somewhere warm, and this destination promised to be much warmer than gloomy England.

By day, they'd used the *G2*'s supersail, alternating to the regular sails during the night, since the supersail required more crew members to manage it. But even though the supersail was only in use for half their travels, the *G2* was zipping through the Atlantic.

"What's that?" Goldie asked.

"It's called a sextant," Minty said.

"Why?"

"Because this little curve at the bottom is a 60-degree angle, or one-sixth of a circle," Minty said.

"What does it do?"

"Well, I'm not exactly sure I can explain—"

"I can," Snowy said, walking up with First Mate Carter. "But it would be better if I could show you under the stars. It's been cloudy every night since we set sail, but it looks like it'll finally be clear tonight."

"Does that mean I can stay up late?" Goldie asked, her soft hazel eyes widening with excitement.

"Well, I guess it wouldn't hurt," Minty said, looking at Snowy. "It *is* for educational purposes."

Carter chuckled. Goldie clapped her hands and skipped off, inviting Clem and Rogers to race her.

Minty watched them and smiled. She was glad they'd been able to rescue Goldie and the others from von Brock's factory. It made her miss her own mother, in a way. But she was grateful for the time she'd been able to spend with Goldie. Looking after someone else almost made her feel like her own mother had never disappeared when the ogres came.

Snowy took the sextant from Minty and ran her fingers over it. "I'd forgotten that I'd asked the men at the Royal Observatory if they could help me with celestial navigation. But I guess they took my letters and forwarded them to Sir Isaac Newton. I was asking about the possibility of building some type of gadget that would measure the angle between the horizon and the stars."

"So that's why the duke brought it to us," Minty said.

"Yes," Snowy replied. "But, unfortunately, it's not completely accurate."

"How so?" Carter asked.

"I'll show you tonight," Snowy said.

***

As the moon rose in the clear, silvery sky, Minty, Snowy, Goldie, and Carter met on the deck. Snowy held up the sextant. "Goldie, I know you don't want to think about the telescope factory."

The little girl shuddered and Minty instinctively pulled her closer.

"But," Snowy continued, "do you remember how mirrors work, especially when you have two of them?"

Minty thought back to how they'd fried Mr. von Brock using his own mirrors and lenses. She could still smell his burning hair at the thought of it.

Goldie nodded, "Yes. You can hold one mirror at an angle so that it reflects what's in the other mirror."

"Right," Snowy explained. "A sextant has two mirrors, and one is what we call half-silvered. That means it has a very thin, reflective coating so it only reflects half the light."

"Why is that?" Carter asked.

"Because otherwise, it would be too bright," Snowy said. "Now, see this little eyepiece?"

Goldie, Minty, and Carter all nodded.

Snowy held the sextant to her eye. "This is the one we look through to see the horizon. You'll notice that it's fixed in place. It's the half-silvered mirror, so we won't be blinding ourselves."

"That would be bad," Carter said with a snort.

Minty laughed.

"Exactly!" said Snowy. "Now, this other little eyepiece-looking thing, down here, see how it swings around?"

The group nodded again.

"This is another mirror," Snowy continued, "but it's full-strength. The light from the object you want to see will reflect off this mirror. So, whether it's the sun or, as I'll show you tonight, a star, you'll see it superimposed on the horizon."

"What does superimposed mean?" asked Goldie.

"That means placed over something else, so you can see both," Minty said.

"Oh."

"Minty," Snowy said, "point the sextant toward this group of stars to the west that looks like two intersecting lines."

Minty looked. "I see them!"

"Focus on the brightest star," Snowy instructed, "and move the arm until it's superimposed on the horizon."

"Got it," Minty said with a grin.

"Now," Snowy said, "with the arm in place, we read the angle off the scale to determine the distance."

"Is it me or do these stars look like—"

"They do form a cross," Snowy said. "It's called the Northern Cross, and it's a group of six stars. It never dips below the horizon at or above 45 degrees north latitude."

"What does latitude that mean?" Goldie asked.

"Well, for reference," Carter chimed in, "London is 51 degrees north latitude. I've seen the Northern Cross everywhere I've sailed, except in winter. It's comforting, especially on long nights, to know that the cross is always there, watching over me."

"Johan Bayer wrote an atlas, called *Uranometria*," Snowy said, "and in it he suggested that three of the stars form one part of the cross, two form the other, and the sixth star represents the body of Christ."

Goldie nodded and yawned.

"Oh, little one, let's get you to bed," Minty said, taking her below deck and tucking her in.

***

In the morning, the sun was bright, and Goldie came running up to Minty, who was just taking the helm.

"Good morning!" she squealed. "I liked learning about the sextant."

"Good morning to you," Minty said, brushing Goldie's straight, dark hair out of her eyes. "Snowy says we still have to make some adjustments."

"Why?"

"That's how we learn," Minty explained. "It's always good to observe and then make improvements based on those observations. It helps make things more accurate."

"Good morning," Snowy said, coming up from below the deck and walking toward Minty and Goldie with a map tucked under her arm.

"I was just telling Goldie how we continually make adjustments as we learn," Minty said, helping Snowy unroll the map.

"That's right," Snowy said, looking at the horizon. She pushed her glasses up her nose. "Hmm."

"What?" Minty asked.

"Well, here's a good example," she said. "According to this map, we should be approaching some islands, but I don't see any—"

"LAND!" Carter called out from the crow's nest, a spyglass to his eye. "We're coming up on land!"

{ **two** }

Kali stepped out of his hut as a light morning drizzle began hitting the mud. He let his toes sink into the soft, damp earth, feeling grounded on his precious land. He inhaled deeply, filling his lungs with the scents of the lush, green landscape and the warm sea air. With a blanket of humidity grazing his shoulders, a sweet, musty odor wafted from the nearby grasses. Their stout stalks whipped back and forth, releasing their fragrance on the wavering breeze. A trio of toads croaked nearby, hopping over the puddles that had begun to form as the rainfall picked up.

For centuries, Kali's ancestors had ruled this land. Rolling hills in the center gave way to terraced plains that sloped toward the surrounding waters. A thick layer of limestone coated most of the island, the result of calcifying sea life skeletons. Like that limestone crust, Kali and his people were hardy and enduring, at once both occupants and elements of their island.

"We are part of this land as much as this land is part of us," he remembered his grandmother telling him when he was small. And that's why he always took care to treat the land with kindness. Wise in the medicinal arts like her, he had been using the island's natural herbs and plants ever since he was a young man.

He took only what he and his family needed, being careful to stay on the innate paths and not trample the native flora. As an exchange of mutual respect, the land offered nutritious vegetation and sheltering shade.

But recently, strangers had appeared, coming on tall ships, pledging friendship and good faith. Kali had been suspicious of their intent. There was something unsettling about these visitors.

One was a man named Jameson, who had proclaimed himself the mayor of an area near Kali's home. How could someone who hadn't been born on this land be capable of ruling it?

However, Jameson had assured Kali that no harm would come to him or his family. The visitors merely wanted to study the native people, and perhaps teach them some things as well. They invited them to share meals and asked them for advice on hunting and working the marsh-like soil on the island.

From the beginning, Kali had insisted that Jameson and his party not cross certain boundaries, as these were sacred areas that were pertinent to his community's beliefs. To this, Jameson gave his word, and Kali was grateful he had been so agreeable.

Kali took a few steps toward the gentle grade where the terrain morphed from muddy bog to a field of the sweet grass, as his family called it. From here, he could see the calm blue waters to the south and west of the island, where a ship with an enormous sail dotted the horizon.

His pulse quickened.

More visitors. I wonder what they want?

Now on alert, he hurried to get a better view of this unusual ship. But before he could get to the rocky outcropping that sat at the edge of his land, he heard a loud noise behind him, followed by yelling.

Kali whipped around just in time to see a large Baobab tree crash to the ground. A sliver of cloudy skies cut through the green foliage, marking the spot where the tree once stood. Kali heard several men shouting what sounded like directions, and then more men swinging away with axes at the tree's thick trunk.

Forgetting the ship in the water, Kali raced past his hut, toads hopping out of the way as he ran through the mud.

"What are you doing?!" he shouted as he neared the fallen tree. Its pale, waxy petals and their puffy purple stamens were scattered on the ground among piles of verdant leaves.

Several men with axes stepped back, holding them across their bodies. As Kali approached, he saw Jameson.

"What are you doing?" Kali repeated, catching his breath.

"We needed to clear this area in order to put up a building," Jameson sniffed.

"But we had an agreement," Kali said, his eyes wide with disbelief.

"That no harm would come to you, your family, or any of the people living here on this island," Jameson explained. "It's only a tree. No one has been harmed."

"That tree is sacred to our people," Kali explained. "We use it for medicine, to keep us in good health, and to provide energy and sustenance."

"There are other sources of food on this island," Jameson said. The men with the axes looked around, uneasy as Jameson held his hand up, signaling for them to wait.

Kali looked at the petals on the ground, soaked with rain. "Do you know how long it takes for a tree to grow to this size? The Baobab trees live for a thousand years. And you've destroyed it in a matter of minutes."

"Besides we need this wood, both for burning and for constructing this building," Jameson said dismissively. "This was the largest tree, so we took this one. Would you have preferred that we chopped down several, or just the one?"

Kali felt his fists ball up as Jameson spoke. "You will regret this," he hissed. "There is magic here, and you have no idea what you're doing. You are playing with fire."

Jameson dropped his hand and the men went back to chopping the Baobab's trunk.

As they did, Kali turned and ran toward his hut. A blistering inferno coursed through his veins, propelling him to run faster than ever before. He stopped in front of his hut, stumbling in the lopsided puddles. The mud was teeming with toads now. He stretched out his arms and tilted his head back, looking straight up at the sky. Fueled by his rage, he recited an incantation. His words spewed out at a furious pace, ascending past the treetops. He closed his eyes. As his spell rose to the drizzly sky, a blazing warmth ignited around him.

{ three }

Snowy noticed flashes of light, brilliant orange flames, and wafts of dark smoke rising from the island the *G2* now approached. The once sunny sky had drastically darkened in a matter of minutes and everyone was shivering below the curtain of rain that now fell. She peered through her spyglass, counting nearly a dozen fires scattered over the green landscape.

"Minty, what do you make of those fires?" she asked.

"I'm not sure. But they do seem to be clustered together. I think we'll be fine if we come in a little more to the west."

The supersail had been retracted and put away, and the crew was working efficiently to bring the ship to the shore. Minty peered out from beneath her tricorn, discussing with Carter how best to maneuver the ship.

"Let's aim for that stretch of beach where the coast dips in a bit," Minty said, motioning with her hand. "That should give us some extra room in case we need to use one of the wings for everyone to offload."

"And it looks like there's a nice grove of trees nearby," Carter replied, "so we should have some shelter from this rain right away. And, hopefully, avoid those fires."

Snowy watched Minty at the helm, impressed by how much her friend had learned about this ship and its capabilities. Then she looked back at the island.

"That's odd," Snowy said.

"What is?" Minty asked.

"The rain is falling exactly where the fires are. You'd think that heavy rain would extinguish them naturally, but it doesn't seem to be making any difference."

Minty nodded. "It looks that way, doesn't it?"

As the ship approached the shore, Snowy heard several men shouting and struggling, as if there were a battle going on. The closer the ship came to the shoreline, the louder the noise. Minty carefully steered the *G2* into position, using the steam thrusters to align it perfectly to the shore, and at last they came to rest. After many weeks at sea, Snowy realized, it felt a bit odd to be idle.

She gathered her notebook and pushed her glasses up her nose, eager to deboard. But the noise coming from the island gave her pause.

"Are they ... fighting?" she wondered aloud.

"That's what it sounds like," Carter replied. He took a rifle and instructed the crew to do the same. "And I don't like the sound of that."

"Me neither," said Minty, her rifle slung against her hip.

Carter, Rogers, Clem, and several of the other men had gathered at the ship's railing, letting down the gangplank and waiting to deboard.

"I'm scared," Goldie began to cry.

Minty kneeled down and brushed back the little girl's hair. "Don't worry," she said. "From now on, it's Snowy, Minty, and Goldie, forever."

Snowy smiled. "That's right."

They lined up with the men and got off the ship, their feet touching dry land for the first time in months. Snowy had nearly forgotten what it felt like. In fact, everything about the island seemed foreign. So many lush green trees and flowering plants surrounded them. Even though they lived in Epping Forest, this kind of vegetation was unfamiliar. But before she could take it all in, the smell of smoke captured her attention. And the yelling was growing louder.

"Come this way," Carter called, leading their group to a clearing under a cluster of trees. "Hurry!"

Snowy scrambled up the gentle slope to the clearing, thankful to be out of the rain. Minty held Goldie's hand and Carter helped the two of them to a dry spot.

"Listen," Carter said, holding his fingers to his lips.

Snowy could hear the shouting more clearly now.

"This is OUR land," an angry voice called out. Even in anger, there was a sing-song quality to the voice. "You have no right to be here!"

"You can't stop us," shouted another voice—this one with a British accent—followed by grunts and groans, landing punches, and other sounds of combat. And, Snowy noted, the din of croaking frogs.

Minty pulled Goldie close. Snowy exhaled. "Oh dear," she said. "What should we do?"

"I think we need to split up," Carter said. "It'll be more effective."

"What?" Minty exclaimed.

"Carter's right," Snowy said. "We can cover more ground that way. We have a signal lantern and a regular lantern in our bags, plus a knapsack of food, and some rope. That should hold us for a while."

"I'll take Clem, Rogers, and the others back to the ship. We can easily sail around to the other side of the island and make some observations from there. It's about noon right now. Let's say we signal each other in four hours."

Snowy looked up toward the sun, but the air was thick with smoke. Then she remembered that the sextant also had a small clock on one side. "Sounds like a plan," she said. "We'll go up this way, keeping to the west, until we can move inland and get high enough up to see what's happening."

"And we'll swing around to the east," Carter said, "then move toward the center of the island."

"Perfect," Snowy said. "Let's see what's causing these fires and all this shouting."

With that, the men headed back to the beach and boarded the ship. Snowy and Minty took Goldie and headed west along the island's shore and then cut into the forest to provide cover. Every now and then, they could see flames and smoke. Goldie was scared, but Minty and Snowy reminded her how brave she'd been in defeating Mr. von Brock.

Snowy's stomach clenched at the sound of the fighting, though. She wasn't sure what they might find when they got to higher ground.

{ four }

Kali held a thick branch from the felled Baobab tree in his hand, ready to strike, as Jameson's men moved into position. He and some of the villagers had begun to battle the unwelcome visitors, with skirmishes breaking out all over the island. Both sides had already suffered injuries, intensifying the fight over this land that was sacred to Kali and his people. But now that his incantation had unleashed an army of loyal soldiers, he wasn't worried about these intruders getting too close.

One by one, and then two by two, the toads from the muddy puddles had morphed into giant men, until they rose from the sludge in droves. With webbed feet and thick thighs, they had bulging eyes and ridged, warty skin on their dark green heads. At nearly seven feet tall and carrying spears as they walked on their stubby hind legs, they were an imposing force. Kali watched them form a barrier around him, confident they would obey his commands.

"What in God's name are those?" a man from Jameson's contingent yelled, ogling in disbelief and backing away.

Kali gripped the Baobab branch and delighted in watching fear fill the eyes of his opponents. He felt the warmth from one of the nearby fires, also the results of his incantation, and was at peace knowing that he'd rather watch his sacred land burn than to give it up to outsiders. The rain lifted the scent of the sweet grass into the air, creating an aroma of burning sugar and blood-spattered mud.

As Jameson's men approached, Kali's toad men stood firm, spears at the ready.

"We were happy to let you live here peacefully," Kali called out. "But you have taken advantage of our kindness and overstepped your boundaries. You were warned that this land was not to be compromised. That was our agreement."

A man in a long dark coat stepped forward, holding up his hands. "My name is Neville Cartwright, and I implore you to listen to us so that we can resolve this without further bloodshed."

The toad men remained motionless, poised to attack on Kali's command.

"Why should I listen to you, Cartwright?" Kali said from behind the phalanx of standing toads. "We told you not to build here or destroy our land, and you've done it anyway. You've proven that your word is no good."

"I understand why you might feel that way," Cartwright said, his arms shaking as he held his hands aloft. "Please, I know we can come up with a solution if you'll just listen."

A fly buzzed near two of the toad men at the front of the line and they both flicked their tongues out to snag it, but it flew away.

"I don't trust you," Kali explained. "Everything you say is a lie."

"No, no," Cartwright pleaded. "That's not true. We only want to *help* you."

"We don't need your *help*," Kali said firmly. "We have been fine without any help for generations before now, and we will be fine without any help for generations to come. You can tell Jameson he is no longer welcome here. We want you to leave our island while you still can."

Again, the fly circled the toad men and this time one of them caught it with his tongue, pulling it into his mouth. This caused Cartwright and his men to shudder.

"Or what?" a voice called from behind Cartwright. "What will you do? Fight us with your overgrown frogs?"

"We're not afraid of you!" another voice called out.

Cartwright's eyes widened and sweat began forming on his brow. The toad men started croaking, their angry chorus rising in the rainy air.

"You do not want to find out," Kali warned.

Then three of Jameson's men pushed forward, colliding with two of the toad men, who quickly wielded their spears to defend themselves. The air was thick with a palpable tension and Kali prepared for battle, tightening his grip on the Baobab branch.

"STOP!" Cartwright shouted. "STOP! I order you to STOP!"

His men stood down, lowering their weapons and breathing heavily. But they remained on alert.

"We will not solve anything with violence," Cartwright said, exhaling.

Kali still didn't trust the man, and he glared at him from behind his army of amphibious soldiers.

"Leave this island," he said, in slow, deliberate tones. "Today."

"I'm afraid we cannot do that," Cartwright said, "but surely we can come to an agree—"

But Kali had heard enough of these empty promises. "Then suffer the consequences you have brought upon yourselves," he said. "This is your final warning."

{ five }

Snowy dabbed her glasses on her sleeve, trying to dry the raindrops and wipe off the condensation that was fogging her vision. It had been a full day since they separated from Clem, Carter, and the rest on the beach at Bridgetown. Now it was late afternoon and they were approaching what she believed to be the trail toward the island's center. She needed to focus on the little path winding through the thickening forest as she, Minty, and Goldie continued their journey. The terrain was sloping upward, and it was getting muddy underfoot. From the sound of it, the fighting they'd heard yesterday had ceased, and the smoke from the fires seemed to be dissipating. But her stomach was still tight.

With careful steps, they climbed the slippery ground, hoping to get a better look at the island's layout. There were many interesting trees and vivid foliage, but she was hesitant to stop and observe the environment for too long. At least the green canopy overhead was deflecting most of the rain.

"Mushrooms!" Goldie called out as they passed a cluster of pale fungi. They were stacked together in neat layers, overlapping each other like the scales of a fish, and they protruded from the ground in a column where their stems were attached to a central core. "What kind are they?"

Minty looked at the cluster. "Those are called oyster mushrooms because the cap is shaped like an oyster," she explained. "They have a faint anise, or licorice smell. And see these gills?"

She pointed to the thin threads attached to the underside of the caps and running down the individual stems. "Those are called decurrent gills."

Snowy raised her brows, causing a few lingering raindrops to run off her glasses. She had forgotten that Minty knew so much about mushrooms, having studied many of the species in Epping Forest and adding them to her tasty creations.

"Can we eat them?" Goldie asked.

"They are edible," Minty said, "but to be honest, I would avoid eating any kind of mushroom that's not familiar."

"And we still have food," Snowy pointed out, hoisting her knapsack. "We'll be fine."

They continued heading up the winding slope and as they got to a clearing, the breeze picked up. Now another scent caught Snowy's attention. "Something smells kind of ... musty," she observed.

They were higher up now and could see more of the island, laid out like a patchwork quilt done in various shades of green and brown, bordered by turquoise waters and crowned by a mix of gray and white clouds. Minty pointed to a field of long stalks below them.

"That's why," she said. "Sugar."

Goldie tilted her head. "Sugar?"

"Well, sugar cane," Minty said. "Before you can spoon it into your tea or add it to your cake, it grows on those stalks. It has to be cut, separated, and boiled before we use it as table sugar."

"It sounds like a lot of work to change the sugar cane into table sugar," Goldie said.

"That's because it is," Snowy said, climbing up a stony path to get a better view of the island, then helping Goldie and Minty up so they could stand beside her and take in the expansive view. "Hard work."

"Wow," Goldie said.

For a moment, Snowy wasn't worried about fires, or smoke, or whatever conflict was happening on this island. All she knew was that she was surrounded by natural beauty. But the sun was getting low on the horizon and the breeze had turned cold.

"It's about to get dark," Snowy said. "Minty, are the lanterns still dry?"

Minty patted the bag she'd been carrying. "I think so."

"I say we make camp there," Snowy said, pointing to a cluster of trees, "and then in the morning, we can make our way down. We'll need to signal Carter tomorrow evening before meeting back at the beach."

"I wonder how he's doing," Minty said.

***

Carter had dropped Clem and Rogers off in an area known as Bathsheba Beach, on the island's east side, before pointing the *G2* toward Bridgetown again. Clem and Rogers had worked their way west, cutting toward the center of the island. On their trek, they'd discovered several gulches that filled with rainwater, making for marshy conditions when the intermittent rain fell. Otherwise, they were mostly dry, built on the thick limestone crust that covered most of the island.

As they progressed further inland, they came upon a grove of tall, unusual trees. They had squatty, thick trunks, with wide branches that looked like roots, and dark green leaves. Frilly, ivory flowers with purple centers hung from the rootlike branches and swayed in the breeze, like the frothy tulle skirts of ballerinas.

"What are those?" Rogers asked.

"I can't be sure," Clem said, "but I think they're Baobab trees. I heard about them years ago from one of my old ship captains. Long before your time. They're known as the Tree of Life."

"Very unusual," Rogers noted.

Clem nodded as the rain began falling again, muddying the men's boots as they trudged along. Soon, a chorus of croaks filled the air, growing louder. As they began to enter a clearing, Clem stopped, his mouth falling open.

"Now *that* is unusual," he said.

He and Rogers watched as a group of toads lined up and jumped into a pond just beyond the clearing. One by one, they went below the water as the other toads waited their turn. And one by one, they emerged on the other side of the pond, transformed into towering amphibious men. Clem and Rogers watched in disbelief as the toad men lumbered along on two hind legs and disappeared into the Baobab grove.

***

As dawn stretched across the cloud-splattered sky, Kali inhaled the fresh, damp air. It seemed to settle him, slowing his heart rate which had been escalated ever since the confrontation with Jameson's men. He inhaled again and closed his eyes, noting the scent of the sea air and the gentle rustling of birds in the Baobabs, going about the business of retrieving breakfast for their offspring. Now his pulse was even and calm. Kali rubbed his forehead, soothing the dull ache that had plagued him since he uttered the incantation. Then he opened his eyes to see the amber streaks of the morning sun glinting from the evaporating puddle, where three small toads sat.

All was peaceful and undisturbed, as it should be. Suddenly sleepy, he went into his hut and laid down for a nap.

The sounds of hammers and shouting men rousted him a few hours later. Kali bolted up, instinctively grabbing a spear from the floor alongside his bedding. He hurried out of his hut and followed the noise, not far from where Jameson's men had felled the Baobab two days ago. He brushed aside the branches lining the path and froze in place when he saw what was happening.

"That's the main wall," a man shouted. "Be sure it's level."

At least a dozen men were attaching countless wooden planks to a series of posts. Just beyond the men lay the fallen Baobab, carved like the carcass of the island's black belly sheep for a feast and then discarded.

Kali felt his heart rate surge. His dark eyes flashed, and his head began to throb again. These visitors had been warned repeatedly, and now their promises had been broken.

From his cover behind the branches, he assessed the scene, noting the number of men and what kind of tools they had. A green monkey chattered from the trees above him and some of the men turned toward Kali. He slunk back and tried to conceal himself.

"Oh, it's splendid," called a voice Kali recognized.

Jameson. That pompous, lying jerk.

He had arrived here under the pretense of helping the islanders, only to proclaim himself mayor and begin making changes without permission. Kali didn't care what that Cartwright man had said. Jameson was clearly in charge and doing harm to this precious land.

"How soon will this be finished?" Jameson asked.

"Walls are going up now," another man said, "shouldn't be too long. Probably get the roof on tomorrow if we can get a break with the rain."

Kali peeked through the branches and saw Jameson nodding as he looked over the men's work.

"Very well," he said. "Keep going."

"Oh, I thought we agreed," said a distressed voice in the background.

Jameson spun around. "Cartwright," he said at the man stepping into the clearing.

"Sir, I beg your pardon," Cartwright said, "but I thought we had agreed to leave this area alone, out of respect for the natives."

"Well, it turns out we need this area," Jameson said.

"But I had an encounter with one of them the other day," Cartwright explained. "His name is Kali, he's their healer."

"The witch doctor," Jameson sniffed.

"I think he might prefer the term medicine man," Cartwright said. Jameson replied with a shrug. "At any rate, he made it quite clear that this area was sacred to the natives for its healing flora and vegetation."

"Well," Jameson said, "they'll get over it. There are plenty of other plants on this island. What we're building will be sacred to us and they can deal with it."

Kali had heard enough. Sweat formed on his brow and he felt his fists clench tightly. He hastened back to his hut and stomped his feet in the mud puddle. Letting loose another incantation, he felt his blood boil inside his skin as he leaned back and howled to the sky. A thick stream of rain descended upon him, filling the empty puddle at his feet with muddy water.

From all directions, toads began hopping into the puddle, and once again emerging at the other end transformed into men ready to do battle. Hundreds of them quickly filed into formation, and with a nod from Kali, they lumbered toward Jameson's men.

When they got to the clearing, the men were frantically trying to finish nailing the last boards of the main wall. But one by one they stopped, surprised to see an army of toad men wielding clubs and branches.

Jameson stepped forward, "What is this nonsense?"

"Sir, I tried to tell you," Cartwright began.

"You have broken your promise!" Kali shouted, working his way to the front of the formation. He glared at Jameson, then carefully placed the tip of his spear against the man's jugular, resting it there, for now. With wide eyes, he calmly explained, "you were warned, but you continued to destroy our land."

Jameson's breath grew thin, a rivulet of sweat dripping from his jaw to his collarbone, where Kali gently applied pressure with his spear.

"We can discuss—"

"The time for talk is over," Kali said, leaning into the spear to emphasize his point. Jameson's breathing became more labored as all his men stood and watched. "Now it is time to die."

"NO!" Cartwright screamed.

One of Jameson's men yanked on his arm to pull him to safety, causing the toad men to react. Kali went to pull Jameson back toward him, but slipped in the mud, giving Jameson a chance to stumble away. With shouts and croaks, a small skirmish escalated into an all-out assault. Bodies were flying and falling, sinking into the mud as the toad men went after Jameson's men.

Meanwhile, the heavens opened, unleashing a torrent of rain on the island. The ground was slick, making it nearly impossible to stay upright. Before long, all of Jameson's men were locked in battle with Kali's toad army, and the casualties were piling up. This was going to be resolved one way or another.

Kali gathered his spear and used it to direct the toad men, imploring them to show no mercy to these invaders. "We must prevail!" he shouted, rallying his soldiers. "Keep fighting! Do not give up!"

{ six }

Meanwhile, after leaving Clem, Rogers, and the others at Bathsheba Beach, Carter had sailed the *G2* back toward Bridgetown. Following the curve of the island's eastern shores, he'd headed south and then continued to head west along the island's southern perimeter. Now he was nearing Bridgetown, and was eager to hear from Snowy and Minty, or the other sailors.

Over the past two days, he'd kept a keen eye out for signals from the lanterns everyone had taken with them. The island was brilliant and green in many parts, with long stretches of pale shoreline. From the crow's nest, he could see the modest mountains and several fields of grasses, as well as jungle-like clusters of trees. It seemed to be a beautiful place, and he wondered what natural elements his friends had discovered. And what kind of dangers they might have encountered. He hoped they'd been adequately prepared for whatever they found.

He went to his quarters and hastily jotted a note.

Arrived Bridgeport. Will wait for signal. Be safe.

~ C.

Then he went to the doves' cage and tucked the note into Evea's collar.

"Soon," he said, patting the bird on the head. She let out a soft coo and then tucked her face back into her feathers, cozying up next to Ivan and going back to sleep.

When he returned to the bridge, he was met by another downpour. He pulled up his coat, which wasn't doing much to shield him against the steady precipitation. The incessant pitter-pat of the raindrops on the deck was beginning to irritate him, but the crash of the waves around the ship helped muffle the sound. The rain had come on so unexpectedly around this place. It was almost as if someone was turning it on and off at will.

With his collar turned up, he sailed farther north and west, pointing the *G2* toward Bridgetown. It wouldn't be much longer now.

"Shall we engage the supersail?" a crew member, Monty, asked, jostling Carter from his thoughts.

"No," he said, "I think we'll make good enough time with this wind behind us."

Carter looked at the island again, surveying the landscape. There still appeared to be fires smoldering all over, sometimes flaring up in large bursts of flames.

"What do you make of that?" Monty said. "Seems odd, doesn't it?"

Carter nodded. "I'm not sure," he said. "Hoping it's just the natives staying warm in this rain, but yes, it does seem unusual that there are so many of those fires, and so spread out."

Monty stood next to Carter on the deck. "If I didn't know better, I'd say there was somewhat of a war going on."

Carter shook his head. "Let's hope not," he said. "We just dealt with war in Europe. This trip was supposed to be a vacation of sorts, just getting away to someplace warm and relaxing."

At that, a huge lightning bolt shot from the sky toward the center of the island, deep within the green cluster of trees. Moments later, a blazing orange fireball lifted over the trees, dissolving into a shower of sparks that fell back to the land.

"Wow!" Monty exclaimed.

Carter gasped. "Oh no! I hope she's, I mean, I hope they're safe."

Monty looked at Carter, then back at the island. "Who's she?"

"Let's engage the supersail after all," Carter said, ignoring Monty's question. "No sense in wasting time. Let's hurry and get to Bridgetown without further delay."

Monty did as he was told and within a few minutes, the *G2* was hurtling along the sea, heading west to Bridgetown. As the crew secured the ship to the dock, Carter went to the cage to release the doves.

"You know what to do," he said. "I just hope it's not too late."

{ seven }

The lightning bolt struck the ground with a flash, showering sparks everywhere and causing Kali to close his eyes. For a moment, he was transported back to his childhood, seeing everything as clearly as if it were happening right in front of him.

"Don't walk there," his grandmother said as they traveled through the Baobab grove, holding his hand on their way to retrieve fresh water from the spring. She gently nudged him to get his feet back on the muddy path next to her.

"Why?"

"You're crushing the plants," her melodic voice softly chided.

"So?"

His grandmother stopped and sighed, her braided, silvered hair bobbing as she shook her head. A colorful fabric stretched over her upper body, wrapped at her waist and extending over her shoulders. "My child," she said, "we need the plants to survive. You must respect them and everything that grows. The trees provide shade in the summer, shelter from storms, and wood for our fires in the winter. The grasses are food for the sheep, which we then eat ourselves. But most importantly, the plants provide medicine, so that we can continue to thrive and be strong enough to ward off those who come to do us harm."

Kali's eyes widened. "Those who come to do us harm?"

At only five years old, he had never known of anyone coming to this island, to do harm or anything else. All he knew was that his family had lived there for many generations, and that they were respected in their community, especially his grandmother. She had the gift of healing, many believed, and people from all over the island came to see her when they were ill or near death. Some, she could save. When she couldn't, she said their time had already come and it was out of her hands.

"Yes, child," she said, "I have seen this in a dream. Men in tall ships. They will come to our land with pretty words, speaking of friendship and offering help. But beware. They are not to be trusted."

Kali drew back in fear. "And what will these men do?"

His grandmother shook her head again. "I do not know," she said. "My dream always ends before I find out. But I am fearful that they will try to take this land from us, at any cost, and destroy what we have built for centuries."

He nodded, trying to get used to the idea that anyone might want to hurt his family.

"Kali," she continued, squeezing his hand, "I want to tell you something. It's time you knew."

He listened intently, staring into her dark eyes, which had begun to look cloudy as she advanced in age. "What is it, Grandmother?"

"You are a special boy," she said, putting her hand on his shoulder and patting it. "You have a gift that you don't know about yet. But I have seen it in you as surely as I have seen it in myself."

"What kind of gift?" He anxiously thought about what he might possibly possess that would be considered a gift. His family lived modestly, in a hut. They weren't wealthy, but they worked hard and always had enough. There never seemed to be a need for anything else.

"You have the gift of healing, child," she confided. "A most valuable gift, indeed."

He straightened his shoulders and stood tall. "Healing?"

"Yes," she said, brushing back her braids, "one day, not long from now, I will be gone."

He frowned. All his young life, he had felt especially close to his grandmother. Though he had brothers, sisters, and cousins, she seemed to favor him over all the others. The thought of losing her upset him.

"No, child, don't be sad," she explained. "Death is part of life. We may not welcome it, but we should not be afraid of it, either. But one day, I will be gone. And our village will need another healer."

He held his breath and whispered, "Me?"

She smiled, her delicate jaw relaxing into a wide grin. "Yes, Kali, you," she said. "I saw it in the stars the night you were born. I knew you had this gift. It is my job to pass on what I have learned and teach you my ways before I depart this life for the next."

He looked around, noting the variety of plants and trees, as if seeing them for the first time. How could he possibly learn about all of them?

"Don't worry," his grandmother said, pulling him to her soft, fleshy hip and hugging him. "We still have plenty of time. You see that soursop tree, for example?"

She pointed to a tree with bumpy, green fruit and Kali nodded. He knew the inside to be creamy-colored, with large, dark seeds and a flavor like pineapples or strawberries.

"We use the fruit and the leaves to get rid of stomach pain," she explained. "Sometimes, it can be used to take away fever, or to help people relax. I like to use it when someone has an infection from swimming in unsafe waters."

As they walked toward the stream, she continued to educate him, answering questions and helping him learn about the healing powers the plants, so abundant on this island, contained. And, she taught him about spells and incantations, and how they could be used to ward off evil.

Within six months, however, she was gone. She had been in declining health, but she was still capable of taking her daily trip to the stream for water, which Kali often made with her. This was her classroom and he was an eager pupil, absorbing as much knowledge as he could on their walks. The day she died, Kali was playing with the other boys his age and told her to go ahead without him.

"Are you sure?" she asked. "I can wait."

"No," he said, chasing the boys, "I'll go tomorrow."

"All right, my child," she said. "Perhaps I'll see you tomorrow."

As she left, she looked back at him. He stared at her and then went back to playing. After several hours, when she hadn't returned, Kali and his father went to look for her. Less than a mile away, they found her at the bottom of a ravine. From what they could figure, she had slipped on a muddy rock, fallen into the ravine and hit her head.

"She died instantly," Kali's father comforted him. "There was nothing anyone could've done."

Kali was riddled with guilt. If only he had gone with her, she might not have slipped. From that day forward, he isolated himself from his family and the other kids in his village, vowing to carry on his grandmother's legacy.

As the sparks showered around him, he opened his eyes. His toad army was ready and waiting. He drew back his spear to prepare for battling, having a final thought.

These are the visitors from my grandmother's dream. I must not let them take our land.

{ eight }

Snowy patted the little matchbox inside her pocket. Ari was safe and dry in there. The rain was falling steadily again, making the rocks slick as they tried to climb the mountain. From what Snowy could tell, this was the highest peak on the island, and should give them an excellent vantage point. She, Minty, and Goldie would be able to see the entire island, if she had calculated correctly, as well as the cause of the fires. And, if the skies were clear enough, she hoped to be able to spot the *G2*, docked near Bridgetown with Carter waiting for the signals from their lanterns.

By now, Snowy hypothesized, Clem should be working his way around the lowlands, heading west from the island's eastern coast. With any luck at all, they'd be able to meet somewhere in the middle.

As they neared the pinnacle, Snowy saw an enormous bolt of lightning descend on the trees below.

"OH!" she exclaimed, caught off guard by the dazzling flash.

Minty hoisted herself up, carrying Goldie on her hip, to stand next to Snowy on the rocks. She looked up at the sky, then waited.

"That's odd," Minty said.

"What is? The lightning?"

"No," Minty said, pausing for another moment.

Snowy wiped the rain splatters off her glasses. "Then what?"

"Hear that?"

"Hear what?" Snowy said, getting flustered.

"I don't hear anything," said Goldie.

"Exactly," Minty said with a confident smile. "No thunder."

Snowy's shoulders dropped. "Ohh," she said, nodding as she realized what Minty was getting at. "Oh, you're absolutely right. That is odd."

She looked around the island. As expected, she could see most of it. They appeared to be near the center, high above the terrain. Everywhere she looked, she could see trees and greenery, with the ocean beyond the pale shoreline that surrounded the space. There were various fires, just as they had seen the other day, some with high flames and others barely smoldering.

"I think we can see more if we get up a little higher," Minty said.

"Race you!" Goldie said.

"Be careful, those rocks look slippery," Snowy cautioned.

"We'll be fine," Minty replied, nearly skipping up the path with a newfound energy, trying to stay ahead of Goldie. "I bet we can see the ship if we get up high enough."

Snowy patted the matchbox in her pocket again and scrambled up the path to catch up to the others. Momentarily, her foot slipped on a muddy rock, causing Snowy to gasp as she looked over the edge. It was a sheer drop into a ravine.

"Oh!" she cried as she caught herself. "Minty, slow down. I don't want to fall."

"Where is it?" Minty said.

"The *G2*?"

Gingerly, Snowy climbed up to the peak, wiping the rain from her glasses every few steps. She wanted to be absolutely certain she could see where she was going. Minty reached out and pulled her up the last two steps.

"Yes, see for yourself," Minty said, pointing to the southwestern horizon. "It should be right down there."

Snowy expected to see the tall mast of the *G2*, bobbing along as if it were at port, but there was nothing. And the view was mostly unobstructed. She turned and looked around the perimeter of the island, searching for the ship somewhere in the ocean. But again, there was nothing.

"I don't understand," she said. "Unless we're just not up high enough. But you'd think we could see it from here."

Minty let out a heavy sigh, "I guess."

Snowy put her arm around Minty. "I know you're disappointed, but just have faith. It'll be there when we need it."

Then a loud, rumbling noise silenced Snowy.

"Thunder?" she asked. "That took long enough."

"It's not thunder," Minty said, motioning to Snowy and Goldie to be quiet. "Listen."

The sound grew louder, rising from the greenest part of the forest below. Snowy narrowed her eyes and listened. It sounded like men yelling, and … toads croaking.

"Do you hear that?" Snowy asked. "It sounds like—"

"Toads," Goldie said, completing Snowy's thought.

Snowy looked at Minty, confused and a little frightened. "Right. But, how many toads are there, and how big are they?" she wondered.

"Exactly," said Minty, who suddenly looked pale as she pulled Goldie closer to her.

The trio crept toward the edge of the mountain, holding onto each other, and straining to listen more carefully. The rumbling noise grew louder, punctuated by angry shouts. Snowy felt her breathing getting shallow. The rain pelted her face, soaking the lenses of her glasses. Her vision obstructed, she tried to push her glasses up her nose. A sudden movement in her peripheral caused her to turn her head quickly. It seemed like the shadows of two birds were hovering nearby.

"OH!" Snowy said, startled by the mysterious image.

Minty reacted by jumping back. "It's Ivan and Evea," she said, extending her arm to provide a landing spot.

But the ground was soaked from the rain, and Minty lost her balance. Holding onto each other, all three of them slipped and fell, hurtling down the side of the mountain toward the ravine below.

***

As they tumbled down the side of the mountain, Snowy, Minty, and Goldie screamed. They bumped into random tree branches, one after the next. As they plummeted toward the rain-drenched ravine below, Minty conked her head on a rock and quickly drifted off to sleep.

"Be careful," her mother warned, as Minty climbed the big rock near their cottage in Epping Forest. "You don't want to fall down and hurt yourself."

"I won't," five-year-old Minty said, her auburn hair in pigtails. She climbed farther up the rock to get a good look at the slug inching its way toward the edge. Fat and slimy, it seemed to be in no hurry to get wherever it was going. Minty was mesmerized as she inspected the way it wiggled at its own leisurely pace.

"Are you going to Snowy's later?" her mother called from the window.

"Yes," Minty said, eyes still on the thick yellow slug. It was the color of wax beans and Minty was equally intrigued and repulsed by its blob-like, oozing form and the slick trail it left in its wake.

"Will you bring her mother the embroidery hoop she loaned me, and two of the little handkerchiefs I made with it? They're on the dining table. And express my thanks for her kindness and generosity."

"Sure," Minty said, barely paying attention. "I'm going to bring her some currant scones, too. The ones I made yesterday."

"That sounds lovely. But don't be long," her mother said. "It's going to start getting dark soon now that autumn is on its way."

The slug had reached the end of the rock but instead of stopping, it plodded on, disappearing over the edge. Minty slid on her stomach, following the slug. She scooted herself up to the edge, watching it as it clung to the underside of the rock. With her legs dangling freely, she pushed up on her hands and leaned over as far as she could.

Now her head was upside down and she adjusted to the view as her pigtails hung loose. Her eyes narrowed as she focused on the slug. Still clinging to the underside of the rock, it pushed itself forward with a slight wobble.

Right into the netlike, circular pattern of a spiderweb.

Minty gasped, astonished that the slug had unwittingly fallen prey to a large brown wolf spider, with pointy legs like scissor blades and eight eyes, arranged in three rows. It was camouflaged perfectly beneath the rock, calmly awaiting its unsuspecting victim. The slug was trapped, unable to slide in the silk-spun web. It wriggled in place, but it was no use. The spider crept toward its plump captive on eight thin legs. Sweeping forward, it methodically began to bind the slug which had already ceased to struggle.

Getting lightheaded, and nearly dizzy from hanging upside down for so long, Minty watched, fascinated, as the spider secured its next meal. With one hand, Minty carefully reached under the rock, stretching her fingertips until she could touch the outer boundary of the spiderweb. She knew from experience that the silk the spider spun from its spinnerets to capture its prey would be soft and fine. But the rest of it would be sticky for the purpose of trapping whatever wandered into it. She'd seen many spiderwebs in Epping Forest, most of them abandoned. But although the spiders themselves made her a bit uncomfortable, she always appreciated the beautiful patterns they spun.

Her face turned red and the top of her head felt heavy. The slug had stopped moving altogether and was likely dead or pretending to be, as a last hope to escape its peril. What a juicy treat this spider was about to enjoy for its feast, Minty thought.

In the late summer sunshine, the moisture built up between her other palm and the surface of the rock. She tried to scoot closer, engrossed in the spider's actions as it circled around its prey. Minty's head was completely inverted now, and she struggled to keep her balance. She grunted, trying to push herself forward again. But just as she got close enough for a good view of the spider, her hand atop the rock began to slip, and she tumbled over the edge, summersaulting in the air and landing in a heap.

{ **nine** }

"Minty, did you hear me?" Snowy said, "Are you all right?" Minty blinked, opening her green eyes after a few minutes.

"Minty," Snowy repeated, "are you all right? You hit your head when we fell."

Minty blinked again and raised her head. She groaned and tried to roll over.

"No, don't move," Snowy said. "We landed in some netting. This is the biggest hammock I've ever seen, if that's what it is. But I'm not sure how long it will hold us. We were so lucky. This netting kept us from hitting the bottom of the ravine."

Minty looked down and shuddered.

"I bumped my knee," Goldie said, sniffing back tears.

"Yes," Snowy said, "but I think you'll be fine, little one. It looks like just a scrape. Can you be brave and help me take care of Minty?"

Goldie stopped crying and nodded.

Minty blinked again. "Oh, my head," she said, reaching up to touch it.

"You smacked it pretty good when we fell off the mountain," Snowy said.

"Mountain?" She looked around. It was chilly and wet, with a canopy of green leaves and vines overhead. "I could've sworn we were in Epping with my—oh. Oh, right."

Snowy gave Minty a quick onceover. "You're not bleeding. Nothing seems to be broken. I think you just gave everything a good whack."

At once, she remembered Ari inside her matchbox. Snowy pulled it out and saw Ari, fast asleep, then tucked the matchbox back in her pocket.

"Now," Snowy continued, "we have to figure out how to get out of this netting. I see there's a cave just up there, along the side of the mountain. This net seems to be suspended just below the opening to the cave. I'm hoping we can crawl up the net and make our way inside. What do you think?"

Minty nodded, "Sure. I think I can do that."

"We can go as slow as you need to," Snowy said.

"I want to race," Goldie announced.

"Oh no, little one," Minty said with a tiny smile. "We're not racing right now."

Snowy was glad Minty was feeling better and the three of them made their way to the side of the net, crawling on their stomachs. The netting had to be twenty-five feet wide by twenty-five feet deep, and it was sticky to the touch. Snowy figured it was from the rain, and she wanted to wipe off her hands but kept going. As they neared the entrance to the cave, she stopped.

"Do you hear that?" she asked.

"Like a hissing noise," Minty replied.

Goldie's lip quivered. "I'm scared," she said, and she started to cry again.

Minty brushed Goldie's dark hair back and gave her a squeeze. "Shh, we'll be fine," she said. "You just have to have faith. We've come this far. Don't be afraid."

As Minty comforted Goldie, Snowy tried to pull herself up the side of the net, using the mountain's warps and grooves for footholds. The noise had stopped, and she was nearly at the entrance to the cave when she looked down. It was still a long drop the ravine, which looked like it had plenty of boulders and broken tree branches inside. Falling into that seemed dangerous. They'd been so fortunate to have landed on this cargo net, or whatever it was. Someone was truly looking out for them.

She turned her attention back to the cave, huffing and grunting as she tried to pull herself up. But the sticky netting and the rain on the side of the mountain had made it difficult to get a solid grip. Her fingernails scraped down to the nub and she began to slip.

"Snowy, try swinging to the other side, toward the middle of the cave's entrance," Minty said from below where she was cuddling Goldie.

"I'll have to let go of the net," she said.

"You can do it," Minty encouraged. "You're strong."

Snowy set her jaw and swung her legs as far as she could, pressing her feet against the mountainside, then worked her upper body over. Though her stomach was fluttering, she maintained her balance. Her arms felt heavy as she let go of the net. Then she reached up to get a higher grasp, finding a dent in the slick mountainside, and then another. After slowly working her way up, she was within a few feet of the cave's floor now.

Suddenly, a loud hiss came from the cave and Snowy froze.

She looked up to see several long, skinny gray legs, covered with hair, advancing toward the cave entrance.

No wonder this hammock is so big, she thought. *It's not a hammock at all. It's a spiderweb, and this must be the spider who spun it.*

Snowy shrieked and dropped to the netting below. It held her weight, but she bounced down, pushing the entire spiderweb dangerously close to the ravine. Minty and Goldie started screaming, too, as they all bounced in the air. They landed in the middle of the web, tumbling for a bit.

"There's a huge spider up there!" Snowy called out. "We can't go up. We'll have to get down. But we're in the middle of the web. We can't climb!"

"I've got it!" Minty exclaimed.

With that, she withdrew the penknife she kept in the secret pocket inside her dress.

"Get the packs," Minty instructed. "I'm going to cut a hole and then we'll have to jump."

"But the ravine is full of branches and boulders," Snowy countered.

"It's our only chance," Minty said.

Snowy knew she was right. She looked up and saw the spider, who had now moved to the cave's entrance. It was as big as a draught horse, at least six feet tall. Though its hairy gray legs were long and thin, its body was plump and thick. It had shiny black eyes and it rubbed its two front legs together as it looked down on them.

Snowy quickly gathered the packs and looked back at Minty, who was wielding her penknife.

"Hurry!" Snowy cried.

Minty thrust her knife into the web, but the silky strands were too strong to be sliced in a single cut. She began to saw back and forth.

Snowy looked up again to see the spider inching closer to the edge of the mountain, perhaps ready to drop into the web.

"Oh, do hurry, Minty!" Snowy screamed, causing Goldie to cry louder.

"I'm trying!" Minty said, working the penknife against the silk. Slowly, the silk began to tear. Snowy closed her eyes, hoping Minty would cut through the web in time.

"WAIT!"

{ ten }

Minty stopped sawing through the web momentarily and looked up at the giant spider filling the entrance to the cave.

Did that thing really just talk?

"Wait!" he repeated. "Don't go. And please, don't cut through my web. I worked so hard to make it."

Goldie clung to Minty, tears streaming down her face as she let out loud sobs.

"Don't cry, little girl," the spider said, with the melodic phrasing in his voice that was common among the islanders.

Goldie sniffed back her tears, infatuated by the large arachnid and its ability to speak.

"A spider that speaks the King's English," Snowy said, pushing her glasses up her nose and looking over at Minty.

Minty shrugged, perplexed by the whole scene.

"Well, I don't know about your king, but yes, I speak English," the spider said, then let out a deep, hearty laugh. "I also speak Portuguese, Spanish, French, and Dutch. It helps to be able to communicate with those who have come here. Like you, why did you come here?"

Minty looked back at Snowy, wondering if she should cut them loose and take their chances jumping into the ravine, or if this giant, talking spider wasn't so dangerous after all. Snowy looked at Minty, and Minty looked at Snowy, and they exchanged a wink. By now, Minty knew that this meant to follow Snowy's lead.

"Well, Mr. Spider, we're on an adventure," Snowy began. "I mean, I'm sorry, what is your name?"

The spider blinked his large black eyes.

"You have a name, don't you?" Snowy asked.

The spider shook his head. "No one has ever given me a name," he said.

"I bet we can fix that," Snowy said with a knowing smile. "My name is Snowy, and these are my friends, Minty and Goldie. We're very pleased to meet you."

That's right, thought Minty, *befriend him and lay on the charm.*

The spider twitched. "I'm very pleased to meet you, too, Snowy, Minty, and Goldie. This will be my first time eating someone whose name I know. Usually, I just eat nasty, nameless pirates and the occasional toad man—"

Minty's brows raised. "Toad man," she said under her breath.

"But," the spider continued, "with all this rain we've been having, I haven't had much to eat."

Goldie began crying again and Minty tightened her grip on her penknife.

"Well," Snowy said, "we can help with that, too. You don't have to eat us, uh, Silky."

"Silky?" the spider said.

"Sure," Snowy replied. "I think that's what we'll call you, since you've spun such a beautiful silky web. It must've taken hours. Do you like that name?"

The spider set back on its long, thin back legs, and a smile stretched across his face, illuminating his black eyes. "I think I do," he said. "But, I'm still very hungry. Maybe just one of you?"

Goldie screamed and Minty squeezed her. "Shh," Minty said. "Don't be scared."

"But I need to eat," Silky emphasized. "And you are my captives."

Snowy snapped her fingers, "Oh, I think I know someone who might be able to help," she said, reaching into her pocket. She pulled out the matchbox. "This is our friend, Ari."

As soon as Ari emerged, crawling across the lid, Silky began to shrink. Minty couldn't believe her eyes. He had shrunk to the size of a common house spider, no longer intimidating. She felt Goldie's grip ease as they all sighed in relief. Then they scaled the net, helping Goldie up with a boost, and met at the entrance to the cave.

"Silky," Minty said, "how did you do that?"

"I have always had the ability to grow or shrink, depending on what the situation dictates," he said, crawling up to Ari. The two of them seemed to be conversing in some secret spider language.

"What the situation dictates?" Minty asked, confused.

"Yes," Silky explained. "Sometimes I need to get very small so I can escape from someone who might want to hurt me. And sometimes I need to make myself bigger to scare them away."

Goldie smiled at Silky and Ari, watching them crawl side by side on the ground.

"Well, you certainly scared us," Snowy said. "But I hope you know we didn't want to hurt you."

"I realize that now," Silky said, "and I can see that you are kind to spiders, from your friend, Ari here. Most people aren't. But the problem is that I don't always know what someone might do. Everyone likes to squish spiders. That's why, when I think I'm in danger, I tend to make myself bigger. I'm harder to squish at that size."

Minty laughed, and so did Silky. Then Snowy and Goldie joined in.

"Are you in danger often out here?" Minty asked.

"Well, not until recently," he said. "I don't know what's been happening, but for the last week or so, there has been much more activity. I see more people than I used to. And there's a lot of noise, trees being cut down, hammers and saws going. Oh, and the rain has been much heavier and frequent than usual."

Snowy looked over at Minty. "What do you make of that?"

Minty shrugged. "I honestly have no idea."

Silky continued, "As I said, with all the rain, I haven't had much to eat."

"Oh, yes!" Snowy said, clapping her hands together. "We have food." She reached into one of the packs and set some dried fruit on the ground. Silky immediately went to it and started eating.

"Thank you," he said between bites. "I'm sorry to be such a bother."

"Nonsense," Minty assured him. "We're happy to share."

"Since you have been so kind," Silky said, "I will release you, if I can join you on your adventure."

"I don't see why not," Minty said.

Silky ate for a while, then stopped.

"Would you like to crawl inside?" Snowy said, holding open the matchbox. "It's warm and dry in there."

"Oh, yes, thank you." Silky crawled into the box with Ari alongside him, and Snowy slid it into her pocket.

Minty looked at Snowy. "That was interesting," she said, rubbing the back of her head, which was still throbbing from earlier. "Now, let's figure out how to get back to Bridgetown. We'll need to hurry so we can meet—"

A noise from the shrubs outside the cave entrance silenced her.

Footsteps.

The leaves parted and Minty grabbed her penknife again. Then she squinted so she could focus on the figure coming into view.

***

"Clem!" Snowy called out as their old crew member stepped into the clearing. "Oh, it's so good to see you!"

Minty fell back, and Snowy caught her.

"Did you faint?" Snowy asked.

"I was dizzy," Minty said. "Maybe I just got too excited."

Clem and Rogers hurried to the cave's entrance. "What happened," Clem asked. "Minty, are you hurt?"

"We slid down the mountain, and she banged her head," Snowy explained.

"And we met a giant spider named Silky," Minty added.

Clem raised his brows. "I'm going to check you out."

Clem had some medical training from his days in the Royal Navy after it was restored in 1660. Though he loved the sea, military life and the trauma that came with it had made him weary. The chance to sail on the *G2* was a welcome respite from armed conflict. And his numerous years of experience made him a valued and respected member of the crew.

"Let's take a look," he said, helping Minty sit up and checking her over. "Tell me, does anything hurt?"

She blinked. "Not really," she said. "Well, the back of my head, a little."

"Yes, you're going to have a bump there," he said. "Follow my finger." He then moved it from side to side, watching her eyes. Satisfied, he announced, "You'll be sore, but I'm happy to report that you appear to have escaped any major injuries. Just take it easy, young lady."

Snowy smiled. Clem had always been like an uncle to her and Minty, so kindly and respectful.

"I'll try," Minty said.

"We really did meet a giant spider," Snowy explained. "And he can grow or shrink to any size. I have him in the matchbox with Ari."

Clem looked skeptical. "Of course you do. That seems about right for what we've seen today."

Snowy and Minty laughed, then Goldie burst out into giggles.

"And hello, little one," Clem said, scooping up Goldie in his arms. "It's good to see you."

Goldie hugged him and then Rogers.

The rain was tapering off, and Snowy heard croaking in the distance. Suddenly, Clem and Rogers stood at guard.

"What is it?" Snowy asked.

"As I was about to say, you won't believe what we saw," Clem said. "In fact, I can barely believe what we saw."

"Me either," said Rogers, who was holding Goldie and looking over his shoulders.

Minty's eyes grew wide. "What was it?"

The noise had stopped, and Clem relaxed while Rogers kept watch.

"Well, your giant spider isn't the only odd thing about this place. When we were coming up the terrain we heard lots of croaking," he began.

"We heard that, too," Snowy said, "from up on the mountain."

"Yes, it was extremely loud," Clem continued. "And we didn't realize how close we were until we came around a bend. The rain was getting thicker and the ground was soaked with puddles. As we were walking, we saw several tiny toads. They hopped off when we approached. I didn't think anything of it at first, except that there seemed to be a lot of them. But when we got closer, we saw this odd, purple glow."

"Purple?" Snowy said.

"Yes, purple," Clem explained.

"More of a glimmer, really," Rogers piped up, still keeping a watchful eye on the brush.

"Right," said Clem. "All around the water. So, these toads, they started jumping into the puddles. But when they'd come out on the other side, they had transformed into—and I can't believe I'm saying this—into amphibious men."

Minty and Snowy gasped.

"What?" Minty asked.

"What does amphibious mean?" Goldie asked.

"Something that can live on land or in water," Snowy explained.

"As I said, I wouldn't have believed it if I hadn't seen it myself," Clem said. "They hopped out on the other side and then started growing in size, larger and larger, until they were about seven feet tall, and walking on two legs."

"OH," Snowy exclaimed. "Then what?"

"Well, it wasn't long before we were discovered," Clem said. "Rogers and I, we fought off as many as we could. They're mean and really pack a wallop, armed with sticks. Some went on to join in the fighting that I'm sure you could also hear from the top of the mountain. Some dispute between the natives and those who sailed here. They chased us back this way. I think we lost them, or maybe they just went on to join the others. Either way, we wanted to hurry and see if we could find you, before they, well—"

Minty shivered. "Oh, I'm so glad you did."

"Me too," said Snowy. "What do you suppose we should do?"

"We need to keep heading west," Clem said. "I think Carter should have the ship in place by now."

They gathered their packs and Snowy checked to make sure Ari and Silky were still tucked snugly into the matchbox. Then Minty and Clem flashed their lanterns, hoping Carter was in position. Finally, the the group of five worked their way west, descending the rest of the mountain, and nearly reaching sea level.

After about an hour, they heard more croaking. Snowy froze, especially frightened now that she knew these were no average toads. Additionally, she could hear men yelling and the sounds of struggle. Minty held Goldie tight.

"You girls stay close," Clem said. Then he motioned to Rogers, who was bringing up the rear.

Coming into a clearing, Snowy could see the violence unfolding ahead. She counted 125 of these amphibious creatures. They were tall with webbed feet and thick legs, each of them with the pale green head of a toad. Goldie drew back in fear, burying her head against Minty's dress. The toad men were wielding sticks, just as Clem had described. Snowy guessed the others were the townspeople, fighting back but clearly outmatched. They appeared to have barricaded themselves within the walls of the city, but some of the toad men had used their sticks and random tree limbs to construct ladders and were jumping over the walls to fight.

Meanwhile, the remaining toad men stood in formation. Snowy squinted to see what they were surrounding. It was a man, draped in brightly patterned cloth, his hair in long, gray braids, falling nearly to his waist. He tilted his head back and looked to the sky.

"I command you to reclaim what is rightfully ours!" the man yelled, and the toad men continued to fight.

They were nearly at the shore now, and Snowy spotted a small boat. "Come on!"

They ran to the boat and jumped in. Instinctively, Snowy started paddling, with Rogers taking the other set of oars. They worked their way around to a nearby pier, which had a couple buildings, including what appeared to be a large warehouse. As they rowed up to the dock, several townspeople gathered around them in a panic.

"What can we do to help?" Snowy said as they disembarked.

"Talk to the mayor!" one man said. "Mr. Jameson will know what to do."

As the rest of the group got off the boat, the mayor approached.

"Mayor Jameson," Snowy said, "we're here to offer our assistance."

He looked her up and down, clearly skeptical.

"Don't let her age, or the fact that she's a girl fool you," Clem cut in. "This is Miss Snowy and Captain Minty of the *Gillfish 2* or as we call it, the *G2*. They're two of the smartest people I know."

"The *G2*?" Jameson said. "Oh, I've heard of your ship. Yes, we'd love some help."

Just then, the toad men burst into sight, wielding their sticks and swinging away at anyone in their path. Snowy and her group fell back.

"Into that warehouse," she said, with Clem, Rogers, Minty, Goldie, and Mayor Jameson scrambling toward the building with her. As she got to the warehouse, she turned and looked. The toad men had rounded up all the townspeople and were marching them toward the large open area between some of the buildings.

"Hurry!" Minty called to Clem, who was fiddling with the lock.

"I've got it," he finally said. "Everyone, get inside!"

Snowy let the others go ahead, then took another look. Two doves circled overhead, and dozens of toad men were headed to the warehouse. She slammed the door shut and locked it. Clem and Rogers pushed some large crates against the warehouse door. Snowy ran to the far side and looked out the window.

"There has to be a hundred of them," she said. "We're surrounded."

{ eleven }

Kali watched as Jameson and several others, including what appeared to be three young girls, scrambled into the building near the pier.

Go ahead and run in fear, he thought. *Soon you will meet your fate and suffer the consequences for having invaded and destroyed our land.*

While a small faction of his toad men battled the townspeople behind him, the majority were headed for the building. They had played directly into his hands by isolating themselves in this structure. There would be no way to escape. He and his army of toad men had two choices: wait them out, or attack. Either way, they had the advantage. And he wasn't in a hurry to decide how this would all play out. No sense in rushing a predetermined fate.

Kali was satisfied in knowing that the spirits of his ancestors would be with him and his amphibious warriors, guiding them through this battle. He thought about his grandmother, how proud she would've been to see him leading his troops to victory. Protecting the integrity of the land she revered and had taught him to respect and value as well.

"We've done nothing wrong!" a man behind Kali yelled, causing Kali to spin around and look. Some of the townspeople were fighting back against his human toads. "We have every right to be here."

Then two of the toad men raised their sticks and delivered a series of blows to the man's ribs, buckling his knees as he screamed in pain. Though he was on the ground, they continued to beat him without mercy. Kali watched with delight.

Perhaps now you will learn your lesson.

As the man screamed in agony, another man broke free from the toad men and came to his aid. But he was also greeted with sharp blows from the toad men's sticks, meeting the same, bloody fate. A woman spat at one of the toads, and without warning, he slapped her with the back of his webbed hand, knocking her to the ground. After that, there was no more resistance from the townspeople.

Shortly, the toad men forced their prisoners to march back up the path toward one of the open spaces between the buildings. This batch of townspeople joined a larger group that was already there, surrounded by the menacing human toads who were holding their weapons at the ready.

Kali turned back to the large building on the pier. Jameson had called it a warehouse, whatever that meant. He gathered that it was some kind of structure intended to hold equipment or other goods, but Kali couldn't imagine what else they might possibly need. The land provided just about everything. But when these men arrived, they were quite keen on constructing this building. That was fine, since it was on the edge of the land. It was when they started going farther into the forest, jeopardizing trees and plants and healing herbs, that the real conflict began.

But that would be over soon enough, he figured.

Focusing again on the warehouse, he watched his toad men carefully file into rows. Then they fanned out, working their way toward all four sides of the building. In neat groupings, they divided themselves, each squadron taking a position along the building's perimeter, sticks poised. Kali waited until the entire building was surrounded. Then he stepped forward and stood in the area just beyond the building's entrance.

"My soldiers," he said, causing the toad men to focus on him. "My brothers of this island. You have been called to do your duty. To protect this land from invaders and drive out the evil they have wrought upon us. We are assured to claim our victory today. But first we must work together to maintain control over this situation. Right now, our enemies are trapped inside, with no escape. We can wait for them to come out, which will expend less energy. Or we can go on the attack."

At this, the toad men began croaking in unison, jumping on their squatty legs and getting fired up at the prospect of combat. Kali could see one of the girls peering out the window. She looked frightened as she pushed her glasses up her nose. With his nostrils flaring, he glared at her, being certain to make eye contact until she shrunk away from the window.

"I can see that you'd prefer to take action," Kali continued, settling down his amphibious army. "And I like that enthusiasm. But for now, I think we should wait, just a little while, to gain the advantage. The longer they stay in there, the more desperate they will become. We want them at their weakest before we engage in battle. And besides, there are only a few of them, while there are a hundred of us. What good can a few old men and some young girls do against our army?"

Again, the toads began to croak, even more enthusiastic than they were before. Kali could see the windows rattle in the warehouse. He looked closer, hoping to see the young girl's face. But apparently, she was too frightened to look outside. And that told him he had her right where he wanted her.

Soon.

{ twelve }

Snowy pulled away from the window, resting against the wall and closing her eyes. There had to be a hundred of those toad men out there, lining every inch of the warehouse and waiting with their sticks. They seemed to be slowing down, but now night was beginning to fall. And she could hear their random croaking.

What are we going to do?

She tried to think of happier times in Epping Forest, skipping stones in the stream, enjoying the late summer breeze rifling through the meadows, biting into Minty's gooseberry crumble at tea time. These creepy toad men wouldn't be able to hurt her there.

"Miss Snowy," Mayor Jameson said, jostling her from her thoughts, "I hope you've got a plan."

Snowy set her jaw. "Of course I do," she said. "Let's take a look around and see what we have to work with."

The warehouse was dusty, with shelves piled high with various tools and other objects. Some items were stored on the warehouse floor, covered in tarps. Others were just stacked up and pushed out of the way. It was going to take time to go through it all.

"I can help you with that," Jameson said. "We store a lot of things in here. Let me show you."

"Go ahead," Clem said, "Rogers and I will keep an eye on those toads. You take your time and figure it out."

With that, Jameson took Snowy on a tour. There were several coils of rope and various nautical tools, as one would expect given that the warehouse was at the dock.

"When our ships arrive, sometimes they need supplies or tools to do repairs," Jameson explained. "We keep those things here so we can keep them seaworthy."

Snowy nodded and followed him to a set of shelves. "What's that?" she asked, pointing to a thick pile of emerald green fabric.

"That's silk from the Orient," Jameson replied. "There was a ship that sailed this way a few months ago. It stopped here for repairs. Now, normally, we don't put a cost on the work we do. We understand that those who are sailing may not have the means to pay for repair work. So, we have a good Samaritan-like policy to just help out where we can and not charge anything."

"That's generous of you," Minty said. She had laid Goldie down on a small settee and was a few steps behind Snowy now.

"Well," Jameson said, "we try to put ourselves in the other person's shoes, so to speak. Otherwise, they'd be stranded. At any rate, this chap wanted to show his appreciation, so he left us these five large bolts of silk he was transporting, as a way of expressing his appreciation. I assured him it wasn't necessary, but he insisted."

"That was very nice of him," Snowy added as they walked further toward the back of the warehouse. She saw Rogers turn quickly as he looked out the window. Then he waved his hand toward her.

"It's all right," he reassured her. "Just thought I heard someone approaching, but it's only the waves hitting the dock. We're fine."

Snowy sighed in relief as they approached some metal tables.

"Now," Jameson said, moving back a tarp over one of the tables, "we've got some lanterns here, and, if you'll look on the floor behind this table, there are two large barrels of kerosene."

Snowy looked back at the bolts of silk, then returned her attention to the table in front of her. "You know," she said, pushing her glasses up her nose, "I think we may be on to something here. Let's see what else we've got."

Inspired, she pushed on through the warehouse with Mayor Jameson, with Minty right behind her. They came around a corner and Snowy stopped.

"Is that what I think it is?" she asked, filling with glee.

"What?" Jameson asked. "The cannon? We pulled that off a ship that came through here."

Snowy immediately began looking it over. "It's perfect," she said. "How about ammunition?"

"We've got some gunpowder back here," Jameson said, squeezing through a narrow space where two sets of shelves came together. "I'm afraid it's just a small bag, however."

"There's twine," Minty called out from another set of shelves. "Can you use that?"

"Yes," Snowy assured. "Definitely. What else is there?"

"We do have a small boat," Jameson announced, pulling back a tarp from the rear of the warehouse.

Snowy's eyes glinted. "A boat, perfect," she said with a smile. She looked around the warehouse again, inventorying everything in her head.

Silk. Tables. Lanterns. Kerosene. Cannon. Gunpowder. Twine. Boat.

What else would they need to complete this plan that was beginning to form in her head?

"We do have a couple of bellows," Jameson said, backing away from the boat and going down another aisle of shelves.

"We'll need those," Snowy said confidently.

"Rubber tubing," Jameson said from the next aisle.

"Yes, we'll take that," Snowy said. "Good."

But something was missing. Her smile began to sink as she looked around. So close to figuring this out and they didn't have—

"Oh, Minty!" she exclaimed. "What's that?"

Minty pushed an old boat anchor aside on the shelf in front of her and pointed to a stubby object. "This?"

Snowy nodded.

"Looks like," Minty said, reaching out to drag the heavy item toward her. "Some kind of bucket with, let's see …"

Just then, the croaking got noticeably louder. It seemed something had the toad men worked up. Snowy held her breath in anticipation. Then she saw Minty frown.

"I don't think this will help," Minty said.

"What is it?" Snowy asked, struggling to hear above the croaks, which were now increasing in volume and frequency.

"Looks like some rusty horseshoe nails."

Snowy couldn't believe her luck. This was the final element she needed to get them out of this warehouse. She clapped her hands and then rubbed them together. As the croaks grew to a cacophonous roar, she said, "PERFECT. Now, let's get to work. I don't think we have much time."

***

"So, how's this going to work?" Minty asked, nearly having to shout over the toad men's croaks. They were banging on the doors now, and it was starting to rattle the windows. She was nervous that they were going to scare Goldie. And who knew what else they might do beyond that? "What's the plan?"

She saw Snowy glance toward the shaking windows, worried about that amphibious army outside as it grew darker.

"We're going to build a balloon," Snowy said.

"A balloon? Why would we want that and besides, how would we get out of—"

Snowy smirked and pointed to the ceiling. For the first time, Minty noticed the hinges on either side and the large panels overlapping each other.

"Retractable," Snowy said.

"Ohh," Minty said, a smile creeping across her face. "Very clever."

"It will be, if we can pull it off," Snowy said. "We'll have to rely on the little light we have and hope we have enough of this silk to get the job done. And, we'll need to work fast."

She turned toward Jameson, who had walked back to the other side of the warehouse.

"Mr. Mayor," Snowy said, "I'll need all of that silk brought to the middle of the warehouse, and I mean right smack in the center."

Jameson spun around and looked at her, perplexed.

"What?" Snowy asked. "Let's get moving."

"First of all," Jameson said, "Nobody orders me around."

"With all due respect," Snowy said, her nose crinkling up, "we don't have time to waste. We need your help if we're all going to make it out of here."

"I don't take kindly to taking orders from a girl," the mayor sniffed.

"Now look here," said Clem, still posted at the window. "I'm not sure what you did to incur the wrath of these toads, but if you want to survive this, you'd better start listening to this girl and do as your told."

Clem and Jameson exchanged a tense look as the croaking droned on, then Jameson dropped his shoulders. "All right," he said, and he started moving the bolts of silk.

Meanwhile, Snowy had gone through her bag and found a notebook. As she sketched, Minty checked on Goldie. She'd somehow fallen asleep and Minty was hesitant to wake her up. With all that croaking and banging, it was better that Goldie couldn't hear it.

Her sketches complete, Snowy reached into her pocket and pulled out the matchbox. When she opened it, Ari and Silky came forward.

"I have an important project for the two of you," Snowy said. Then she explained that they'd be constructing a balloon from this silk, holding up her sketchbook to show them her plans. "It doesn't have to be pretty. You just have to sew these bolts together."

"But I don't know how," Silky admitted.

"I bet Ari can teach you," Minty said.

Ari crawled toward Silky and began to demonstrate what he needed to do. Soon, the spiders were busy joining the large green bolts into a balloon pattern.

"What's next?" Minty asked, noticing the croaking had died down, for now.

"We need to get that cannon mounted on the boat," Snowy said. "But I can't carry it."

"Rogers, I'll keep watch so you can help Mayor Jameson," Minty said.

"You got it, Captain Minty," Rogers said, exchanging places with her.

Together, the men lugged the cannon to the boat, then mounted it on the very front.

"We're going to need one barrel of kerosene in the middle of the boat," Snowy explained. "Then load the cannon with the gunpowder, and all the rusty nails we can fit inside there."

Minty's brows raised. "Rusty nails?"

"We're going to have one shot," Snowy said. "God willing, that's all it takes."

The sky was nearly black now, and the croaking and banging had subsided. But Minty knew, it was going to be a long night. As Goldie slept, everyone in the warehouse was either working, or keeping watch, if not both.

"Let's get the legs off that table," Snowy instructed.

Minty looked around. "I don't see a saw."

"Break them off," Snowy said, her brow furrowed as she pushed on a table leg.

Minty studied the leg and then used all her strength to press against what she figured to be the weakest point. It took a few tries, but she did it. Then she and Snowy worked together until all four legs were broken off.

"Now what?" Minty asked.

"We're going to use that twine to bind these legs to the legs of the other table," Snowy said. "I need it to be taller."

"Are you sure?"

"No," Snowy said, smiling at Minty. "But it's the best plan I've got."

Minty gave her a wink and started unrolling the twine. Then they turned one table on its side, and tied the broken legs to it, doubling its height. They got Rogers and Jameson to help them lift it up.

"Now," Snowy said, "let's slide that other barrel of kerosene under here, and then set those four lanterns on the top of the table. Minty, do you have your penknife?"

"Of course I do," she said.

"I need you to cut two holes in each of the barrels," Snowy instructed. Then she looked out the window, which was showing the faintest light coming from the east. "We'll have our best shot to get this thing up around dawn, since that will be the coolest temperature."

Silky and Ari were still working away, their giant balloon taking shape as it stretched across the four corners of the warehouse. Minty drew her penknife and carefully cut the holes in each of the kerosene drums.

She looked over and saw Goldie stirring on the settee.

"Hello, little one," Minty said.

"What are you doing?" Goldie asked with sleepy eyes.

"We're building a balloon," Minty explained.

"A balloon?"

Snowy came over. "Yes, and I have a very important job for you, when it's time."

Goldie's eyes widened. "What kind of job?"

"I know you like to race," Snowy said. "But can you climb?"

Minty frowned. She wasn't sure climbing was such a good idea for Goldie.

"Sure!" Goldie said.

"Great," Snowy said. "You see the panels on the ceiling, and that long ladder that leads up to the bridge? I need you to scramble up there and undo all the latches on those panels. Then they can slide open."

"Why?"

"So we can open it," Snowy said.

Minty felt her stomach tumble. The thought of having Goldie up there made her nervous.

"I don't think that's such a good—"

"It's the only way," Snowy said. "She'll be able to get up there the easiest. Besides, I need everyone else to get things into place and she's too small to help with that."

Minty nodded, knowing Snowy was right.

"In fact," Snowy added, "Goldie, you can start climbing up there right now if you want. It's going to take a while to work all the way across that ceiling."

Minty watched as Goldie climbed the ladder, gasping under her breath now and then until Goldie was safely at the bridge. She looked down at Minty, who smiled back at her. Then Goldie got to work, undoing each of the latches one by one.

"Now," Snowy said, "let's see how our balloon is coming along. Looks like it's nearly done."

Minty watched Goldie, trying not to worry about her, and then followed Snowy.

"Wow, Silky," Minty said. "You've done a great job with Ari."

"You sure have," Snowy said. "Now, Minty, let's stretch it all the way out."

Minty and Snowy worked at opposite corners to lay the balloon as flat as possible. Then they had Silky spin a super web to attach the balloon to the boat. Minty couldn't believe how quickly he worked. When he was done, Snowy took out the matchbox and ushered the spiders inside. "You've both earned a nice long rest," she said as she tucked it back into her pocket.

Next, they enlisted Mayor Jameson to get the kerosene ready. He fed it into each of the lanterns, which then began filling the balloon. Then Snowy placed some tubing in one of the barrel's holes, while Minty did the same with the other barrel. Then they worked a bellows into the other hole of their respective barrels. This created a swell of hot air and the balloon started filling faster.

"We're pumping this kerosene through pressure," Snowy explained as the balloon filled. "It's working!"

Minty could see the sky's hue turning from inky black to a soft gray. The sun would be rising soon. "Snowy, it's almost dawn—"

But taps on the side of the building silenced the rest of her thought.

"The toad men are awake," Clem announced. "I was hoping they'd sleep a little longer."

Then they all heard taps going up the sides of the building, from all around, and heading toward the roof.

Minty quivered, afraid they wouldn't make it out in time.

"We can do this," Snowy said. "Everyone just listen and get in the boat."

Minty looked up to see that Goldie had made it all the way across the bridge. As the balloon filled, Snowy called out, "Now, Goldie!"

Without hesitation, Goldie pushed on a lever. One by one, a series of the roof panels slid back. Some of the hardware began falling off the building and crashing to the ground outside, taking some of the toad men down with it.

Goldie squealed with delight, but Minty could see one of the toad men crawling along the side of the open roof, heading toward her little friend.

"Goldie!" Minty cried. "Look out!"

He was perilously close, and the balloon began to lift off the floor. With Minty, Snowy, Jameson, and Rogers now inside the boat, Minty held on tight.

"Clem!" Snowy yelled, "we're almost out of kerosene. Push that other barrel out from under the table and get in here!"

Minty watched as Clem followed Snowy's instructions. Then she and Snowy worked the bellows at a fever pitch until the balloon surged upward. As it did, Minty heard glass breaking and looked down. Several of the toad men were now dropping into the warehouse from the windows and were coming toward them.

Then she looked up, where Goldie was waiting on the bridge.

"We're almost there, Goldie!" Minty shouted. "Hang on!"

With a toad man closing in on either side of her, Goldie froze in place. Minty could see that she wouldn't be able to reach Goldie as the balloon continued to lift. The thought of leaving her behind made her stomach flip.

"I've got her!" Clem yelled, reaching all the way over the side of the boat and snatching her just as the toad men approached.

With the green silk illuminated by the rising sun, they sailed up out of the warehouse. Bathed in the pale green glow, Minty looked down once more and saw several of the human toads swarming and hopping around, their croaks filling the air as the balloon began to drift.

{ thirteen }

"NO!" Kali screamed, his fists clenched as he watched the large object float over his head and out of the building. "We can't let them get away!"

His army of human toads was crawling all over the warehouse by now, croaking in a growing frenzy as they piled on top of each other. Those who were upright banged their sticks on the ground, rattling the warehouse walls as more toad men spilled out the sides.

As Kali thrashed his fists in the air, his eyes lit with fire and a loud thunderclap boomed over the island, followed by a dazzling bolt of lightning that filled the dawn sky. The lightning narrowly missed the green object fastened to what he recognized as a boat, which was slowly ascending into the air. He fixed his intense gaze on the mysterious, black metal piece mounted to the boat's bow. As it took flight, he stretched to get a better look. He'd never seen something so bizarre.

Then that lying turncoat, Jameson, peered over the edge of the boat and made eye contact. Kali spewed forth a furious spell, spitting out his words in a fiery burst and fuming that he was going to be denied the opportunity for revenge. This man and his kind had invaded Kali's island, a sacred space full of natural resources for healing and nourishment. They had broken their promises time and again, pledging good will and cooperation. But it was all lies. Instead, their carelessness and false friendship had harmed their environment and the future of Kali's people for generations to come. And now, it was time for them to be punished for the deceitful actions. Kali could think of no more fitting revenge than to watch Jameson suffer and then take his final breath.

Enraged, he focused on the man's pale, fleshy face as the boat continued to climb into the air. Then he began shouting a series of gruesome threats.

"Jameson, your skin will be pierced by sharp-toothed rats, nibbled and torn into shreds. Your hair will become matted and tangled with sandflies who will feed on your tattered flesh. Your eyes will be punctured and chewed by venomous spiders, savoring every moist bite of your eyeballs as they gorge themselves. This is your punishment for your disrespect in coming to our island and harming it forever."

A girl with blonde hair leaned over the side of the boat, standing next to Jameson. Kali shot her a glance and she quickly retreated. Meanwhile, the object wafted back and forth in the air, listing side to side but slowly rising.

The toad men clamored, their croaks and grunts growing in volume. As they piled on top of each other, those at the top of the pile jumped into the air, attempting to reach the boat.

"We need to get higher!" screamed the girl in the boat. "Keep pumping those bellows!"

But the boat continued its slow ascent, and the toad men scrambled to pile up and create a higher platform. Kali watched with pleasure as one of his own toad men narrowly missed the edge of the boat, slipping and falling to the muddy ground, breaking his neck.

The girl in the boat screamed, and Jameson drew back in horror. But soon a new pile of toads had formed, and another, and another. With croaks and grunts, they jumped and flung themselves into the air, reaching the edge of the slow-floating object and then crashing to the ground before stacking up again.

"Get them!" Kali screamed to his toads. "Do not let them escape!"

Several of the toad men piled up, but this time, they brought their sticks. One ascended the stack and jabbed his stick at the bottom of the boat, causing it to sway. On the other side, another toad used a stick to turn the boat in the other direction. Everyone aboard began screaming as Kali let out a wicked laugh. He enjoyed toying with these invaders, knowing they would soon meet their fate. The two toad men banged on the boat's hull and it began to shake violently back and forth.

Kali cackled with delight as the screams and croaks and bangs grew louder.

Then he saw a pair of gray birds soaring in on a light breeze that blew through the palm trees. The breeze allowed the large green orb to pick up just enough momentum to right the boat. As it climbed out of reach, even from the toad men's sticks, Kali shouted to the sky.

"NO!"

***

"Ivan and Evea!" Minty shouted as she saw the doves approach the listing balloon. "That means Carter made it!"

She turned to look westward, toward the ocean. Sure enough, there was the familiar mast of the *G2*, chugging hard and approaching the pier. Her heart swelled and she was filled with confidence that they would be safe.

Minty returned her attention to the small boat and her fellow passengers. They'd been jostled around and terrified by the angry toad men and their sticks. But it seemed everything would be fine now. Though the small boat was righted, its ascent had slowed as the breeze died down. At least they were up high enough that the toads couldn't reach them.

She and Snowy pumped the bellows, but it didn't make any difference in the boat's progress.

"We're running out of kerosene," Snowy said. "I don't know if we'll be able to escape."

"Give the bellows to Rogers and me," Clem said. "I'm sure your arms are tired. Let's see if we can get a better result."

As she handed over the bellows, Minty stroked Goldie's hair. The little girl was quiet but clearly upset. Minty worried that they'd crash after all and succumb to the creepy army of toads waiting below. She peeked over the edge of the boat and saw the man who had been yelling at Mayor Jameson. He was shouting words Minty couldn't understand, angry words that hissed from his lips.

As he spoke, the toads seemed to multiply, and they all worked together to form a single pile. Now they were approaching the bottom of the boat. No matter how furiously Clem and Rogers pumped the bellows, the balloon wouldn't rise any faster. Her eyes filled with dread as the toads approached, hopping on their squatty legs and wielding their sticks. The man on the ground laughed, delighting in her fear.

One sickly green toad croaked in a deep baritone voice and pushed his way up to the top of the pile. He was within reach of the boat's hull, and he drew back his stick, taking aim with precision and ready to thrust it into the vulnerable boat.

BOOM!

Minty and the others rocked back and forth in the boat, falling into one another. She looked over the side to see that Carter had fired the *G2*'s cannons, leveling the pile of toads. Dozens of them lay on the ground, gravely injured. The man continued his angry chanting, and the remaining toads attempted to build another pile.

Meanwhile, the force of the cannon's blast provided just enough wind to push the balloon toward a marsh. Though still flying low, at least they had managed to get farther away. The silky green balloon drifted at an uneven pace, lurching at times. At first, Minty was thrilled.

"I think we're safe now," she said, exhaling in relief.

"I'd like to think so," said Snowy. "But the surrounding trees and the distance from the pier mean that the *G2* is now out of range, should we need another round of cover fire."

Right away, a chorus of croaks came from below. Minty looked over the side and saw a smaller unit of toad men following their balloon.

"Don't forget," Clem said, "we've still got the cannon."

"It's a last resort," Snowy said. "But we may have no choice."

"Jameson!" called the man on the ground. "You must surrender now!"

Jameson, sweaty and breathing hard, peered over the edge of the boat. "I'm not going to do that, Kali," he said.

"Kali?" Minty asked. "Who is this man?"

"He calls himself a healer," Jameson explained. "Some might call him a witch doctor."

Snowy's brows raised above the rim of her glasses. "Witch doctor?"

"Jameson!" the man yelled again.

As Minty moved to the other side of the boat to get a better look, the balloon drifted toward a tree and was snagged on an exposed limb. She and Snowy hurried to detangle the balloon's fabric from the branch, but they had begun to drop.

As the croaking grew louder, Minty saw that the toad men had formed a circle, surrounding the boat.

"Jameson!" Kali yelled once more. "You must surrender!"

"No—" he began, but Snowy interrupted him.

"We accept!" she yelled, causing Jameson to stammer.

"Wh-what are you doing?"

Snowy looked at Minty, and Minty looked at Snowy, and they exchanged a wink. Clem nodded at Rogers and Minty put her arm around Goldie, pulling her close.

"We accept," Snowy repeated, holding her arms in the air. "But you must call off your army. Have them drop their weapons so we can talk."

"I will do no such thing," Kali said, glaring at Snowy. "The mayor never should have double-crossed me. Now he must suffer the consequences and face my soldiers."

"There aren't very many of them left," Jameson said.

"With my magic, I can make more toads," Kali explained with a wicked laugh as the balloon hovered near the tree. "A thousand toad men will feast upon you this very morning if I command them to do so."

With a sharp lurch, the boat rapidly dropped altitude.

"We're out of fuel," Clem said with an eerie calmness. He nodded slowly at Snowy.

Then Jameson turned toward Kali. "Surrender and let us talk, and free our townspeople, or we will be forced to kill you and your toad men."

"Never!" Kali shouted. "We will never surrender. You are on OUR land. And the time for talking is over. Toads, raise your weapons!"

The boat was approaching the ground, its potential landing spot surrounded by stick-wielding toads. Minty's eyes grew wide as she moved into position. She knew what she had to do.

"That's your choice," Snowy said as the boat continued to drift downward, hovering about ten feet in the air by now.

Kali looked at the boat's passengers. He fixed his eyes on Goldie and curled his lips into a wicked smile. "On my count," he said, "impale these invaders! All of them! One! Two!"

BLAM!

A burst of cannon fire shot through the toad men, spraying rusty nails everywhere. One by one, they fell, bleeding. As the smoke cleared, Minty looked up from the cannon's site and saw that her shot had struck Kali squarely in the chest. She swallowed hard, disturbed that she had mortally wounded him.

The boom echoed as the balloon slumped over and the boat gently touched down on the soft marshland. And then there was nothing but silence.

Snowy looked back at Minty.

"Nailed it," Minty said.

The few remaining toad men scattered as the balloon finally collapsed. As Kali took his last breath, the lumbering members of his amphibious armies morphed back into harmless toads.

{ fourteen }

Snowy watched the toads scampering into the edge of the swamp, just a few feet from where their makeshift airship had crashed. One by one, they disappeared beneath the surface, leaving a trail of ripples. As they spread across the swamp, she realized something.

"We have to drain this," she announced.

"What?" Minty asked. "Why?"

"If we don't," Snowy said, stepping out of the boat, "they can regenerate. We need to ensure that they don't come back again."

"I can take care of that," Mayor Jameson said. "We have some very skilled citizens—"

"Oh, the townspeople!" Snowy interrupted. "We've got to free them."

"Already on it," Clem said, stepping over the deflated balloon. "Come on, Rogers."

The pair ran up the bank to the open area beyond the piers and Snowy could see them cutting through the ropes that bound the people of the town. Soon, everyone was freed, and the mayor asked those with building experience to assemble in the town square.

"Before I begin, I want to express our most sincere thanks to Snowy, Minty, Goldie, and their crew for their help. We are lucky to be alive," he said as the villagers broke out in applause. "Now, I need a crew of builders to come forward. We will have two projects that must be completed immediately."

Snowy wondered why he mentioned two projects, not just one. After a group had gathered, the mayor continued.

"First, we need a few of you to change the course of the diversion valves in these swamps," he explained. "After that, we'll begin building rock barriers on the mountain streams. Those will effectively drain this area."

The men in the group murmured among themselves.

"Can I add something?" Snowy asked.

Mayor Jameson nodded, "Of course."

"Thank you," Snowy said. "Another option would be to break down and dig out a portion of one of these ponds, allowing it to drain back to the stream just down the way, and then to the ocean. That might be easier and take less time."

The men murmured again, nodding in agreement.

"That is a brilliant plan," the mayor said. "Now, I bet you're wondering about the second project."

Carter came up the bank, having docked the *G2* nearby. He quietly hugged Snowy, Minty, and Goldie, and shook hands with Clem and Rogers.

Snowy turned back to Mayor Jameson so she could listen.

"I know we came here with a plan to build and create our own life here," he said. "But, we also came here in good faith, and I'm afraid we haven't done a very good job of living our faith. There were people here before we arrived, and we have intruded on an area that is very important to them. So, I am hereby ordering that, effective immediately, we tear down the structure we were building in that area, then wall it off. I want the people who live here to know that they can trust us to respect their land, and that we will not intrude again."

Several of the townspeople exchanged puzzled glances, but one by one, they began nodding and a slow round of applause began to rise.

As the townspeople surrounded the mayor, asking questions about the work to be done, Snowy stepped back from the group. Things seemed to be well in hand. She looked out at the ocean, thinking about her cottage in Epping Forest, and wondering how Claudette and her daughters were doing.

"So," Minty said, coming up beside Snowy, with Carter and Goldie right behind her. "What should we do next?"

Snowy sighed. "Well, this wasn't much of a vacation."

"And it wasn't very warm," Minty laughed.

"Warmer than England, at least," Snowy replied with a shrug.

"It would help if we could rest here, at least for a few days," Carter said. "The ship has been sailing hard and the crew could use a break."

"That sounds—" Snowy began, then paused as she watched something in the ocean.

"What?" Minty asked.

Snowy blinked, not sure if she had seen what she thought she had seen. Maybe all that kerosene and her lack of sleep had gone to her head. She looked back at the ocean, but it was gone.

"Sorry," she said. "That sounds like a good idea."

Then she pulled the matchbox from her pocket and opened it, letting Ari and Silky crawl around on her sleeve. Goldie held out her hand and the spiders crawled onto it. Her mouth fell open as she watched them crawl across her palm. "They're racing!" She spun in a circle and tumbled gently to the ground, fascinated by the spiders.

Clem and Rogers joined the group. "I think these folks might need a little assistance with the building process," Clem said. "Carter, can you come over with us and see how we can help?"

The men walked off and Minty asked Snowy, "What did you see out there?"

Snowy felt cold, which seemed odd with the morning sun still rising in the sky. She shivered and rubbed her hands over her arms. She looked back at the ocean, unable to shake the feeling that she was being watched. Then she turned to Minty.

"Nothing," she said. "Come on. Let's see how we can help."

They each took one of Goldie's hands and walked back to the group. Several yards from the docked *G2*, the waves crashed, and a thick tail disappeared beneath the water.

About the Author

Justin Mitson lives in Garden City, Idaho. A technologist and entrepreneur, he loves to write fun, engaging stories, from children's adventures and mob comedies to deep science fiction and time travel tales. Born in Butte, Montana, he spent most of his childhood roaming around the northwest, living in eighteen different locations before getting through high school. This gave him a sense of adventure and encouraged his imagination. A student of history as well as technology, Mr. Mitson loves to ask, "what if?" When he's not writing, he's an avid water ski and snow ski enthusiast (and occasionally does those two activities on the same day) and loves to ride his electronic skateboard on the miles of the Boise area's greenbelt. Above all, his greatest joy is making his wife and two daughters laugh.

www.ingramcontent.com/pod-product-compliance
Lightning Source LLC
LaVergne TN
LVHW012031060526
838201LV00061B/4548